Harry Potter ™

2002–2003
Student Planner

Cedco Publishing Company
100 Pelican Way, San Rafael, CA 94901
All rights reserved.

AUGUST 2002

Sun	Mon	Tue	Wed	Thu	Fri	Sat
				Last Quarter Moon ◑ **1**	**2**	**3**
4	Holiday (Rep. of Ireland & Scotland) Civic Holiday (Canada except Quebec) **5**	**6**	**7**	New Moon ● **8**	**9**	**10**
11	**12**	**13**	**14**	First Quarter Moon ◐ **15**	**16**	**17**
18	**19**	**20**	**21**	Full Moon ○ **22**	**23**	**24**
25	Late Summer Holiday (U.K.) **26**	**27**	**28**	**29**	Last Quarter Moon ◑ **30**	**31**

SEPTEMBER 2002

Sun	Mon	Tue	Wed	Thu	Fri	Sat
Father's Day (Aust. & N.Z.) **1**	Labor Day (Canada & U.S.) **2**	**3**	**4**	**5**	New Moon ● **6**	Rosh Hashanah **7**
Grandparents' Day **8**	**9**	**10**	**11**	First Quarter Moon ◐ **12**	**13**	**14**
15	Yom Kippur **16**	**17**	**18**	**19**	**20**	Full Moon ○ **21**
22	Autumnal Equinox 12:56 A.M. E.D.T. Canterbury (South) Anniversary (N.Z.) **23**	**24**	**25**	**26**	**27**	**28**
Last Quarter Moon ◑ **29**	Queen's Birthday (W.A.) **30**					

October 2002

Sun	Mon	Tue	Wed	Thu	Fri	Sat
		1	2	3	4	5
New Moon ● 6	Labour Day (A.C.T., N.S.W. & S.A.) 7	8	9	10	11	12
First Quarter Moon ◑ 13	Columbus Day (observed) Thanksgiving Day (Canada) 14	15	16	17	18	19
20	Full Moon ○ 21	22	23	24	Hawke's Bay Anniversary (N.Z.) 25	26
Daylight Saving Time ends (Canada, U.K. & U.S.) 27	Labour Day (N.Z.) Holiday (Rep. of Ireland) 28	Last Quarter Moon ◐ 29	30	Halloween 31		

November 2002

Sun	Mon	Tue	Wed	Thu	Fri	Sat
					All Saints' Day (U.K.) 1	2
3	Marlborough Anniversary (N.Z.) New Moon ● 4	Election Day Guy Fawkes Day (U.K.) 5	6	7	8	9
Remembrance Sunday (U.K.) 10	Veterans' Day Remembrance Day (Aust., Canada & U.K.) First Quarter Moon ◑ 11	12	13	14	Canterbury (North Central) Anniversary (N.Z.) 15	16
17	18	Full Moon ○ 19	20	21	22	23
24	25	Last Quarter Moon ◐ 26	27	Thanksgiving Day 28	St. Andrew's Day (Scotland) Hanukkah 29	30

DECEMBER 2002

Sun	Mon	Tue	Wed	Thu	Fri	Sat
1	Westland Anniversary (N.Z.) 2	3	New Moon ● 4	5	6	7
8	9	10	First Quarter Moon ◑ 11	12	13	14
15	16	17	18	Full Moon ○ 19	20	Winter Solstice 8:15 P.M. E.S.T. 21
22	23	24	Christmas 25	St. Stephen's Day (Rep. of Ireland) Boxing Day (Aust., Canada, N.Z. & U.K.) Last Quarter Moon ◑ 26	27	28
29	30	31				

JANUARY 2003

Sun	Mon	Tue	Wed	Thu	Fri	Sat
			New Year's Day 1	New Year's Holiday (N.Z. & Scotland) New Moon ● 2	3	4
5	6	7	8	9	First Quarter Moon ◑ 10	11
12	13	14	15	16	17	Full Moon ○ 18
19	Martin Luther King Jr. Day Southland Anniversary (N.Z.) Wellington Anniversary (N.Z.) 20	21	22	23	24	Last Quarter Moon ◑ 25
Australia Day (Aust.) 26	Auckland Anniversary (N.Z.) 27	28	29	30	31	

FEBRUARY 2003

Sun	Mon	Tue	Wed	Thu	Fri	Sat
					New Moon ● 	1
2	Nelson Anniversary (N.Z.) 3	4	5	Waitangi Day (N.Z.) 6	7	8
First Quarter Moon ◐ 9	10	11	Lincoln's Birthday 12	13	St. Valentine's Day 14	15
Full Moon ○ 16	Presidents' Day 17	18	19	20	21	Washington's Birthday 22
Last Quarter Moon ◑ 23	24	25	26	27	28	

MARCH 2003

Sun	Mon	Tue	Wed	Thu	Fri	Sat
						St. David's Day (Wales) 1
New Moon ● 2	Eight Hours Day (Tas.) Labour Day (W.A.) 3	4	Ash Wednesday 5	6	7	International Women's Day 8
9	Commonwealth Day (U.K.) Canberra Day (A.C.T.) Labour Day (Vic.) Taranaki Anniversary (N.Z.) 10	First Quarter Moon ◐ 11	12	13	14	15
16	St. Patrick's Day 17	Full Moon ○ 18	19	Vernal Equinox 8:00 P.M. E.S.T. 20	21	22
23	Otago Anniversary (N.Z.) Last Quarter Moon ◑ 24	25	26	27	28	29
Mothering Sunday (U.K.) Daylight Saving Time begins (United Kingdom) 30	31					

April 2003

Sun	Mon	Tue	Wed	Thu	Fri	Sat
		New Moon ● **1**	**2**	**3**	**4**	**5**
Daylight Saving Time begins (Canada & U.S.) **6**	**7**	**8**	First Quarter Moon ◐ **9**	**10**	**11**	**12**
Palm Sunday **13**	**14**	**15**	Full Moon ○ **16**	Passover **17**	Good Friday **18**	**19**
Easter **20**	Easter Monday (Aust., Canada, N.Z., Rep. of Ireland & U.K.) **21**	Earth Day **22**	St. George's Day (England) Last Quarter Moon ◑ **23**	**24**	National Arbor Day Anzac Day (Aust. & N.Z.) **25**	**26**
27	**28**	**29**	**30**			

May 2003

Sun	Mon	Tue	Wed	Thu	Fri	Sat
				New Moon ● **1**	**2**	**3**
4	May Day Holiday (Rep. of Ireland & U.K.) Labour Day (Queensland) **5**	**6**	**7**	**8**	First Quarter Moon ◐ **9**	**10**
Mother's Day (Aust., Canada, N.Z. & U.S.) **11**	**12**	**13**	**14**	Full Moon ○ **15**	**16**	**17**
18	Victoria Day (Canada) **19**	**20**	**21**	Last Quarter Moon ◑ **22**	**23**	**24**
25	Memorial Day (observed) Spring Holiday (U.K.) **26**	**27**	**28**	**29**	**30**	New Moon ● **31**

June 2003

Sun	Mon	Tue	Wed	Thu	Fri	Sat
1	Queen's Birthday (N.Z.) Holiday (Rep. of Ireland) 2	3	4	5	6	First Quarter Moon ☽ 7
Pentecost Whitsunday (Aust., N.Z. & U.K.) 8	Queen's Birthday (Aust. except W.A.) 9	10	11	12	Flag Day Full Moon ○ 13	14
Father's Day (Canada, U.K. & U.S.) 15	16	17	18	19	20	Summer Solstice 3:10 P.M. E.D.T. Last Quarter Moon ☾ 21
22	23	St. Jean Baptiste Day (Quebec) 24	25	26	27	28
New Moon ● 29	30					

July 2003

Sun	Mon	Tue	Wed	Thu	Fri	Sat
		Canada Day (Canada) 1	2	Independence Day 3	4	5
First Quarter Moon ☽ 6	7	8	9	10	11	12
Full Moon ○ 13	Holiday (N. Ireland) 14	15	16	17	18	19
20	Last Quarter Moon ☾ 21	22	23	24	25	26
27	28	New Moon ● 29	30	31		

Class Schedule

1st Qtr

Time	Mon	Tue	Wed	Thu	Fri

2nd Qtr

Time	Mon	Tue	Wed	Thu	Fri

Class Schedule

Time	Mon	Tue	Wed	Thu	Fri

4TH QTR

Time	Mon	Tue	Wed	Thu	Fri

2002

Last Quarter Moon ◑

JULY
S	M	T	W	T	F	S
	1	2	3	4	5	6
7	8	9	10	11	12	13
14	15	16	17	18	19	20
21	22	23	24	25	26	27
28	29	30	31			

AUGUST
S	M	T	W	T	F	S
				1	2	3
4	5	6	7	8	9	10
11	12	13	14	15	16	17
18	19	20	21	22	23	24
25	26	27	28	29	30	31

SEPTEMBER
S	M	T	W	T	F	S
1	2	3	4	5	6	7
8	9	10	11	12	13	14
15	16	17	18	19	20	21
22	23	24	25	26	27	28
29	30					

AUGUST 5 – AUGUST 11

2002

Holiday (Rep. of Ireland & Scotland)

Civic Holiday (Canada except Quebec)

Mon 5

Tue 6

Wed 7

New Moon ●

Thu 8

Fri 9

Sat 10

Sun 11

JULY						
S	M	T	W	T	F	S
	1	2	3	4	5	6
7	8	9	10	11	12	13
14	15	16	17	18	19	20
21	22	23	24	25	26	27
28	29	30	31			

AUGUST						
S	M	T	W	T	F	S
				1	2	3
4	5	6	7	8	9	10
11	12	13	14	15	16	17
18	19	20	21	22	23	24
25	26	27	28	29	30	31

SEPTEMBER						
S	M	T	W	T	F	S
1	2	3	4	5	6	7
8	9	10	11	12	13	14
15	16	17	18	19	20	21
22	23	24	25	26	27	28
29	30					

AUGUST 12 – AUGUST 18

Mon
12

Tue
13

Wed
14

First Quarter Moon ◑

Thu
15

Fri
16

Sat
17

Sun
18

JULY						
S	M	T	W	T	F	S
	1	2	3	4	5	6
7	8	9	10	11	12	13
14	15	16	17	18	19	20
21	22	23	24	25	26	27
28	29	30	31			

AUGUST						
S	M	T	W	T	F	S
				1	2	3
4	5	6	7	8	9	10
11	12	13	14	15	16	17
18	19	20	21	22	23	24
25	26	27	28	29	30	31

SEPTEMBER						
S	M	T	W	T	F	S
1	2	3	4	5	6	7
8	9	10	11	12	13	14
15	16	17	18	19	20	21
22	23	24	25	26	27	28
29	30					

August 19 – August 25

2002

Mon
19

Tue
20

Wed
21

Full Moon ○

Thu
22

Fri
23

Sat
24

Sun
25

July						
S	M	T	W	T	F	S
		1	2	3	4	5	6
7	8	9	10	11	12	13
14	15	16	17	18	19	20
21	22	23	24	25	26	27
28	29	30	31			

August						
S	M	T	W	T	F	S
				1	2	3
4	5	6	7	8	9	10
11	12	13	14	15	16	17
18	19	20	21	22	23	24
25	26	27	28	29	30	31

September						
S	M	T	W	T	F	S
1	2	3	4	5	6	7
8	9	10	11	12	13	14
15	16	17	18	19	20	21
22	23	24	25	26	27	28
29	30					

Late Summer Holiday (U.K.)

Mon
26

Tue
27

Wed
28

Thu
29

Last Quarter Moon ◑

Fri
30

Sat
31

Father's Day (Aust. & N.Z.)

Sun
1

JULY

S	M	T	W	T	F	S
	1	2	3	4	5	6
7	8	9	10	11	12	13
14	15	16	17	18	19	20
21	22	23	24	25	26	27
28	29	30	31			

AUGUST

S	M	T	W	T	F	S
				1	2	3
4	5	6	7	8	9	10
11	12	13	14	15	16	17
18	19	20	21	22	23	24
25	26	27	28	29	30	31

SEPTEMBER

S	M	T	W	T	F	S
1	2	3	4	5	6	7
8	9	10	11	12	13	14
15	16	17	18	19	20	21
22	23	24	25	26	27	28
29	30					

SEPTEMBER 2 – SEPTEMBER 8

2002

Labor Day (Canada & U.S.)

Mon 2

Tue 3

Wed 4

Thu 5

New Moon ●

Fri 6

Rosh Hashanah

Sat 7

Grandparents' Day

Sun 8

AUGUST						
S	M	T	W	T	F	S
				1	2	3
4	5	6	7	8	9	10
11	12	13	14	15	16	17
18	19	20	21	22	23	24
25	26	27	28	29	30	31

SEPTEMBER						
S	M	T	W	T	F	S
1	2	3	4	5	6	7
8	9	10	11	12	13	14
15	16	17	18	19	20	21
22	23	24	25	26	27	28
29	30					

OCTOBER						
S	M	T	W	T	F	S
		1	2	3	4	5
6	7	8	9	10	11	12
13	14	15	16	17	18	19
20	21	22	23	24	25	26
27	28	29	30	31		

Mon
9

Tue
10

Wed
11

Thu
12

First Quarter Moon ☽

Fri
13

Sat
14

Sun
15

AUGUST						
S	M	T	W	T	F	S
				1	2	3
4	5	6	7	8	9	10
11	12	13	14	15	16	17
18	19	20	21	22	23	24
25	26	27	28	29	30	31

SEPTEMBER						
S	M	T	W	T	F	S
1	2	3	4	5	6	7
8	9	10	11	12	13	14
15	16	17	18	19	20	21
22	23	24	25	26	27	28
29	30					

OCTOBER						
S	M	T	W	T	F	S
		1	2	3	4	5
6	7	8	9	10	11	12
13	14	15	16	17	18	19
20	21	22	23	24	25	26
27	28	29	30	31		

Yom Kippur

Mon
16

Tue
17

Wed
18

Thu
19

Fri
20

Full Moon ○

Sat
21

Sun
22

AUGUST						
S	M	T	W	T	F	S
				1	2	3
4	5	6	7	8	9	10
11	12	13	14	15	16	17
18	19	20	21	22	23	24
25	26	27	28	29	30	31

SEPTEMBER						
S	M	T	W	T	F	S
1	2	3	4	5	6	7
8	9	10	11	12	13	14
15	16	17	18	19	20	21
22	23	24	25	26	27	28
29	30					

OCTOBER						
S	M	T	W	T	F	S
		1	2	3	4	5
6	7	8	9	10	11	12
13	14	15	16	17	18	19
20	21	22	23	24	25	26
27	28	29	30	31		

2002

Autumnal Equinox 12:56 A.M. E.D.T.

Canterbury (South) Anniversary (N.Z.)

Mon
23

Tue
24

Wed
25

Thu
26

Fri
27

Sat
28

Last Quarter Moon ◑

Sun
29

August
S	M	T	W	T	F	S
				1	2	3
4	5	6	7	8	9	10
11	12	13	14	15	16	17
18	19	20	21	22	23	24
25	26	27	28	29	30	31

September
S	M	T	W	T	F	S
1	2	3	4	5	6	7
8	9	10	11	12	13	14
15	16	17	18	19	20	21
22	23	24	25	26	27	28
29	30					

October
S	M	T	W	T	F	S
		1	2	3	4	5
6	7	8	9	10	11	12
13	14	15	16	17	18	19
20	21	22	23	24	25	26
27	28	29	30	31		

Queen's Birthday (W.A.)

Mon
30

Tue
1

Wed
2

Thu
3

Fri
4

Sat
5

New Moon ●

Sun
6

A U G U S T						
S	M	T	W	T	F	S
				1	2	3
4	5	6	7	8	9	10
11	12	13	14	15	16	17
18	19	20	21	22	23	24
25	26	27	28	29	30	31

S E P T E M B E R						
S	M	T	W	T	F	S
1	2	3	4	5	6	7
8	9	10	11	12	13	14
15	16	17	18	19	20	21
22	23	24	25	26	27	28
29	30					

O C T O B E R						
S	M	T	W	T	F	S
		1	2	3	4	5
6	7	8	9	10	11	12
13	14	15	16	17	18	19
20	21	22	23	24	25	26
27	28	29	30	31		

OCTOBER 7 – OCTOBER 13

Labour Day (A.C.T., N.S.W. & S.A.)

Mon
7

Tue
8

Wed
9

Thu
10

Fri
11

Sat
12

First Quarter Moon ◑

Sun
13

SEPTEMBER						
S	M	T	W	T	F	S
1	2	3	4	5	6	7
8	9	10	11	12	13	14
15	16	17	18	19	20	21
22	23	24	25	26	27	28
29	30					

OCTOBER						
S	M	T	W	T	F	S
		1	2	3	4	5
6	7	8	9	10	11	12
13	14	15	16	17	18	19
20	21	22	23	24	25	26
27	28	29	30	31		

NOVEMBER						
S	M	T	W	T	F	S
					1	2
3	4	5	6	7	8	9
10	11	12	13	14	15	16
17	18	19	20	21	22	23
24	25	26	27	28	29	30

OCTOBER 14 – OCTOBER 20

2002

Columbus Day (observed)

Thanksgiving Day (Canada)

Mon 14

Tue 15

Wed 16

Thu 17

Fri 18

Sat 19

Sun 20

SEPTEMBER						
S	M	T	W	T	F	S
1	2	3	4	5	6	7
8	9	10	11	12	13	14
15	16	17	18	19	20	21
22	23	24	25	26	27	28
29	30					

OCTOBER						
S	M	T	W	T	F	S
		1	2	3	4	5
6	7	8	9	10	11	12
13	14	15	16	17	18	19
20	21	22	23	24	25	26
27	28	29	30	31		

NOVEMBER						
S	M	T	W	T	F	S
					1	2
3	4	5	6	7	8	9
10	11	12	13	14	15	16
17	18	19	20	21	22	23
24	25	26	27	28	29	30

OCTOBER 21 – OCTOBER 27

2002

Full Moon ○

Mon 21

Tue 22

Wed 23

Thu 24

Hawke's Bay Anniversary (N.Z.)

Fri 25

Sat 26

Daylight Saving Time ends (Canada, U.K. & U.S.)

Sun 27

Slytherin
™

SEPTEMBER						
S	M	T	W	T	F	S
1	2	3	4	5	6	7
8	9	10	11	12	13	14
15	16	17	18	19	20	21
22	23	24	25	26	27	28
29	30					

OCTOBER						
S	M	T	W	T	F	S
		1	2	3	4	5
6	7	8	9	10	11	12
13	14	15	16	17	18	19
20	21	22	23	24	25	26
27	28	29	30	31		

NOVEMBER						
S	M	T	W	T	F	S
					1	2
3	4	5	6	7	8	9
10	11	12	13	14	15	16
17	18	19	20	21	22	23
24	25	26	27	28	29	30

OCTOBER 28 – NOVEMBER 3

2002

Labour Day (N.Z.)

Holiday (Rep. of Ireland)

Mon 28

Last Quarter Moon ☽

Tue 29

Wed 30

Halloween

Thu 31

All Saints' Day (U.K.)

Fri 1

Sat 2

Sun 3

SEPTEMBER
S	M	T	W	T	F	S
1	2	3	4	5	6	7
8	9	10	11	12	13	14
15	16	17	18	19	20	21
22	23	24	25	26	27	28
29	30					

OCTOBER
S	M	T	W	T	F	S
		1	2	3	4	5
6	7	8	9	10	11	12
13	14	15	16	17	18	19
20	21	22	23	24	25	26
27	28	29	30	31		

NOVEMBER
S	M	T	W	T	F	S
					1	2
3	4	5	6	7	8	9
10	11	12	13	14	15	16
17	18	19	20	21	22	23
24	25	26	27	28	29	30

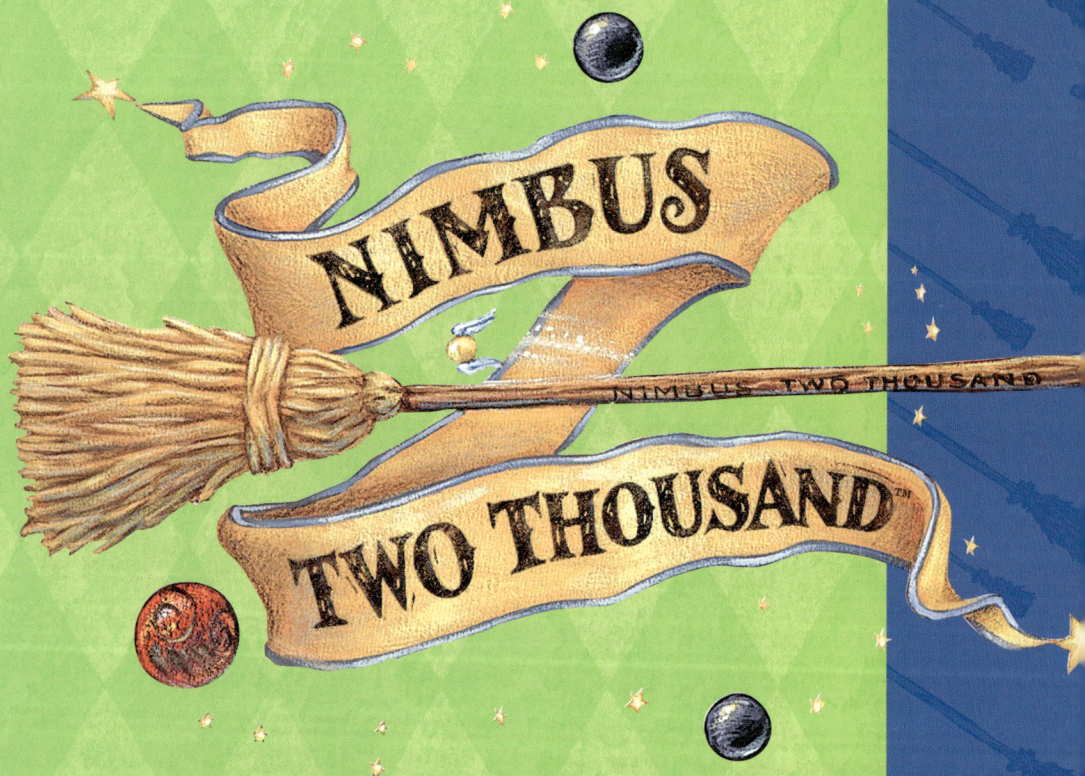

2002

Marlborough Anniversary (N.Z.)

New Moon ●

Mon
4

Election Day

Guy Fawkes Day (U.K.)

Tue
5

Wed
6

Thu
7

Fri
8

Sat
9

Remembrance Sunday (U.K.)

Sun
10

OCTOBER						
S	M	T	W	T	F	S
		1	2	3	4	5
6	7	8	9	10	11	12
13	14	15	16	17	18	19
20	21	22	23	24	25	26
27	28	29	30	31		

NOVEMBER						
S	M	T	W	T	F	S
					1	2
3	4	5	6	7	8	9
10	11	12	13	14	15	16
17	18	19	20	21	22	23
24	25	26	27	28	29	30

DECEMBER						
S	M	T	W	T	F	S
1	2	3	4	5	6	7
8	9	10	11	12	13	14
15	16	17	18	19	20	21
22	23	24	25	26	27	28
29	30	31				

TREVOR

NOVEMBER 11 – NOVEMBER 17

2002

Remembrance Day (Aust., Canada & U.K.)

Veterans' Day

First Quarter Moon ◐

Mon 11

Tue 12

Wed 13

Thu 14

Canterbury (North Central) Anniversary (N.Z.)

Fri 15

Sat 16

Sun 17

OCTOBER						
S	M	T	W	T	F	S
		1	2	3	4	5
6	7	8	9	10	11	12
13	14	15	16	17	18	19
20	21	22	23	24	25	26
27	28	29	30	31		

NOVEMBER						
S	M	T	W	T	F	S
					1	2
3	4	5	6	7	8	9
10	11	12	13	14	15	16
17	18	19	20	21	22	23
24	25	26	27	28	29	30

DECEMBER						
S	M	T	W	T	F	S
1	2	3	4	5	6	7
8	9	10	11	12	13	14
15	16	17	18	19	20	21
22	23	24	25	26	27	28
29	30	31				

November 18 – November 24

Mon 18

Full Moon ○

Tue 19

Wed 20

Thu 21

Fri 22

Sat 23

Sun 24

OCTOBER						
S	M	T	W	T	F	S
		1	2	3	4	5
6	7	8	9	10	11	12
13	14	15	16	17	18	19
20	21	22	23	24	25	26
27	28	29	30	31		

NOVEMBER						
S	M	T	W	T	F	S
					1	2
3	4	5	6	7	8	9
10	11	12	13	14	15	16
17	18	19	20	21	22	23
24	25	26	27	28	29	30

DECEMBER						
S	M	T	W	T	F	S
1	2	3	4	5	6	7
8	9	10	11	12	13	14
15	16	17	18	19	20	21
22	23	24	25	26	27	28
29	30	31				

November 25 – December 1

Mon
25

Tue
26

Last Quarter Moon ◑

Wed
27

Thanksgiving Day

Thu
28

Fri
29

St. Andrew's Day (Scotland)

Hanukkah

Sat
30

Sun
1

OCTOBER						
S	M	T	W	T	F	S
		1	2	3	4	5
6	7	8	9	10	11	12
13	14	15	16	17	18	19
20	21	22	23	24	25	26
27	28	29	30	31		

NOVEMBER						
S	M	T	W	T	F	S
					1	2
3	4	5	6	7	8	9
10	11	12	13	14	15	16
17	18	19	20	21	22	23
24	25	26	27	28	29	30

DECEMBER						
S	M	T	W	T	F	S
1	2	3	4	5	6	7
8	9	10	11	12	13	14
15	16	17	18	19	20	21
22	23	24	25	26	27	28
29	30	31				

December 2 – December 8

2002

Westland Anniversary (N.Z.)

Mon 2

Tue 3

New Moon ●

Wed 4

Thu 5

Fri 6

Sat 7

Sun 8

NOVEMBER						
S	M	T	W	T	F	S
					1	2
3	4	5	6	7	8	9
10	11	12	13	14	15	16
17	18	19	20	21	22	23
24	25	26	27	28	29	30

DECEMBER						
S	M	T	W	T	F	S
1	2	3	4	5	6	7
8	9	10	11	12	13	14
15	16	17	18	19	20	21
22	23	24	25	26	27	28
29	30	31				

JANUARY						
S	M	T	W	T	F	S
			1	2	3	4
5	6	7	8	9	10	11
12	13	14	15	16	17	18
19	20	21	22	23	24	25
26	27	28	29	30	31	

2002

Mon
9

Tue
10

First Quarter Moon ◖

Wed
11

Thu
12

Fri
13

Sat
14

Sun
15

N O V E M B E R						
S	M	T	W	T	F	S
					1	2
3	4	5	6	7	8	9
10	11	12	13	14	15	16
17	18	19	20	21	22	23
24	25	26	27	28	29	30

D E C E M B E R						
S	M	T	W	T	F	S
1	2	3	4	5	6	7
8	9	10	11	12	13	14
15	16	17	18	19	20	21
22	23	24	25	26	27	28
29	30	31				

J A N U A R Y						
S	M	T	W	T	F	S
			1	2	3	4
5	6	7	8	9	10	11
12	13	14	15	16	17	18
19	20	21	22	23	24	25
26	27	28	29	30	31	

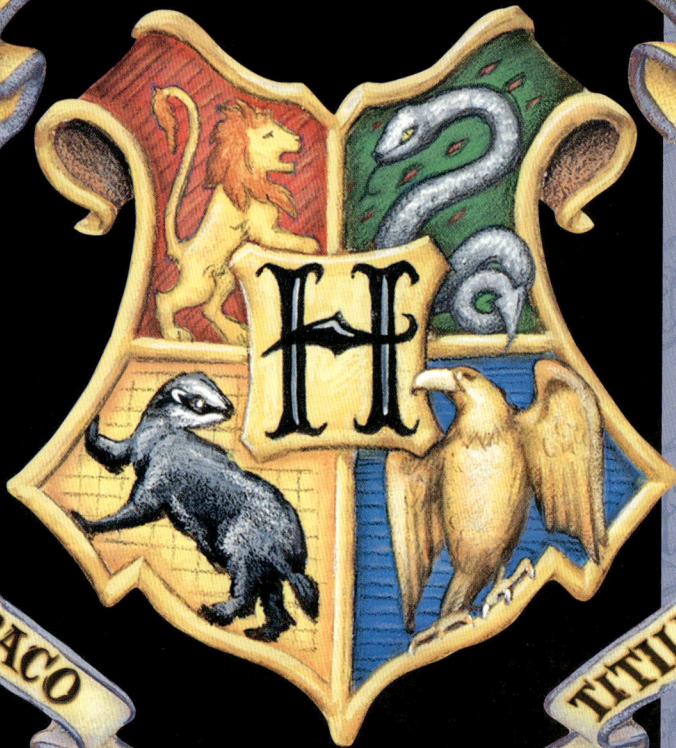

HOGWARTS™

DRACO DORMIENS NUNQUAM TITILLANDUS

Mon
16

Tue
17

Wed
18

Full Moon ○

Thu
19

H

Fri
20

Winter Solstice 8:15 P.M. E.S.T.

Sat
21

Sun
22

NOVEMBER						
S	M	T	W	T	F	S
					1	2
3	4	5	6	7	8	9
10	11	12	13	14	15	16
17	18	19	20	21	22	23
24	25	26	27	28	29	30

DECEMBER						
S	M	T	W	T	F	S
1	2	3	4	5	6	7
8	9	10	11	12	13	14
15	16	17	18	19	20	21
22	23	24	25	26	27	28
29	30	31				

JANUARY						
S	M	T	W	T	F	S
			1	2	3	4
5	6	7	8	9	10	11
12	13	14	15	16	17	18
19	20	21	22	23	24	25
26	27	28	29	30	31	

2002

Mon
23

Tue
24

Christmas

Wed
25

Boxing Day (Aust., Canada, N.Z. & U.K.)

St. Stephen's Day (Rep. of Ireland)

Last Quarter Moon ◑

Thu
26

Fri
27

Sat
28

Sun
29

NOVEMBER						
S	M	T	W	T	F	S
					1	2
3	4	5	6	7	8	9
10	11	12	13	14	15	16
17	18	19	20	21	22	23
24	25	26	27	28	29	30

DECEMBER						
S	M	T	W	T	F	S
1	2	3	4	5	6	7
8	9	10	11	12	13	14
15	16	17	18	19	20	21
22	23	24	25	26	27	28
29	30	31				

JANUARY						
S	M	T	W	T	F	S
			1	2	3	4
5	6	7	8	9	10	11
12	13	14	15	16	17	18
19	20	21	22	23	24	25
26	27	28	29	30	31	

DECEMBER 30 – JANUARY 5

Mon 30

Tue 31

Wed 1

New Year's Day

New Year's Holiday (N.Z. & Scotland)

New Moon ●

Thu 2

Fri 3

Sat 4

Sun 5

NOVEMBER						
S	M	T	W	T	F	S
					1	2
3	4	5	6	7	8	9
10	11	12	13	14	15	16
17	18	19	20	21	22	23
24	25	26	27	28	29	30

DECEMBER						
S	M	T	W	T	F	S
1	2	3	4	5	6	7
8	9	10	11	12	13	14
15	16	17	18	19	20	21
22	23	24	25	26	27	28
29	30	31				

JANUARY						
S	M	T	W	T	F	S
			1	2	3	4
5	6	7	8	9	10	11
12	13	14	15	16	17	18
19	20	21	22	23	24	25
26	27	28	29	30	31	

2003

Mon
6

Tue
7

Wed
8

Thu
9

First Quarter Moon ◖

Fri
10

Sat
11

Sun
12

DECEMBER						
S	M	T	W	T	F	S
1	2	3	4	5	6	7
8	9	10	11	12	13	14
15	16	17	18	19	20	21
22	23	24	25	26	27	28
29	30	31				

JANUARY						
S	M	T	W	T	F	S
			1	2	3	4
5	6	7	8	9	10	11
12	13	14	15	16	17	18
19	20	21	22	23	24	25
26	27	28	29	30	31	

FEBRUARY						
S	M	T	W	T	F	S
						1
2	3	4	5	6	7	8
9	10	11	12	13	14	15
16	17	18	19	20	21	22
23	24	25	26	27	28	

JANUARY 13 – JANUARY 19

2003

Mon
13

Tue
14

Wed
15

Thu
16

Fri
17

Full Moon ○

Sat
18

Sun
19

DECEMBER						
S	M	T	W	T	F	S
1	2	3	4	5	6	7
8	9	10	11	12	13	14
15	16	17	18	19	20	21
22	23	24	25	26	27	28
29	30	31				

JANUARY						
S	M	T	W	T	F	S
			1	2	3	4
5	6	7	8	9	10	11
12	13	14	15	16	17	18
19	20	21	22	23	24	25
26	27	28	29	30	31	

FEBRUARY						
S	M	T	W	T	F	S
						1
2	3	4	5	6	7	8
9	10	11	12	13	14	15
16	17	18	19	20	21	22
23	24	25	26	27	28	

JANUARY 20 – JANUARY 26

2003

Martin Luther King Jr. Day

Southland Anniversary (N.Z.)

Wellington Anniversary (N.Z.)

Mon 20

Tue 21

Wed 22

Thu 23

Fri 24

Last Quarter Moon ◑

Sat 25

Australia Day (Aust.)

Sun 26

Quidditch ™

DECEMBER						
S	M	T	W	T	F	S
1	2	3	4	5	6	7
8	9	10	11	12	13	14
15	16	17	18	19	20	21
22	23	24	25	26	27	28
29	30	31				

JANUARY						
S	M	T	W	T	F	S
			1	2	3	4
5	6	7	8	9	10	11
12	13	14	15	16	17	18
19	20	21	22	23	24	25
26	27	28	29	30	31	

FEBRUARY						
S	M	T	W	T	F	S
						1
2	3	4	5	6	7	8
9	10	11	12	13	14	15
16	17	18	19	20	21	22
23	24	25	26	27	28	

2003

Auckland Anniversary (N.Z.)

Mon
27

Tue
28

Wed
29

Thu
30

Fri
31

New Moon ●

Sat
1

Sun
2

DECEMBER						
S	M	T	W	T	F	S
1	2	3	4	5	6	7
8	9	10	11	12	13	14
15	16	17	18	19	20	21
22	23	24	25	26	27	28
29	30	31				

JANUARY						
S	M	T	W	T	F	S
			1	2	3	4
5	6	7	8	9	10	11
12	13	14	15	16	17	18
19	20	21	22	23	24	25
26	27	28	29	30	31	

FEBRUARY						
S	M	T	W	T	F	S
						1
2	3	4	5	6	7	8
9	10	11	12	13	14	15
16	17	18	19	20	21	22
23	24	25	26	27	28	

2003

Nelson Anniversary (N.Z.)

Hufflepuff

™

Mon
3

Tue
4

Wed
5

Waitangi Day (N.Z.)

Thu
6

Fri
7

Sat
8

First Quarter Moon ◐

Sun
9

JANUARY						
S	M	T	W	T	F	S
			1	2	3	4
5	6	7	8	9	10	11
12	13	14	15	16	17	18
19	20	21	22	23	24	25
26	27	28	29	30	31	

FEBRUARY						
S	M	T	W	T	F	S
						1
2	3	4	5	6	7	8
9	10	11	12	13	14	15
16	17	18	19	20	21	22
23	24	25	26	27	28	

MARCH						
S	M	T	W	T	F	S
						1
2	3	4	5	6	7	8
9	10	11	12	13	14	15
16	17	18	19	20	21	22
23	24	25	26	27	28	29
30	31					

FEBRUARY 10 – FEBRUARY 16

Mon 10

Tue 11

Wed 12

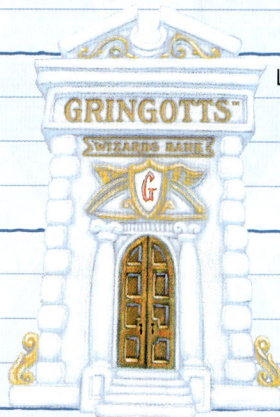

Lincoln's Birthday

Thu 13

St. Valentine's Day

Fri 14

Sat 15

Full Moon ○

Sun 16

S	M	T	W	T	F	S
			1	2	3	4
5	6	7	8	9	10	11
12	13	14	15	16	17	18
19	20	21	22	23	24	25
26	27	28	29	30	31	

FEBRUARY

S	M	T	W	T	F	S
						1
2	3	4	5	6	7	8
9	10	11	12	13	14	15
16	17	18	19	20	21	22
23	24	25	26	27	28	

MARCH

S	M	T	W	T	F	S
						1
2	3	4	5	6	7	8
9	10	11	12	13	14	15
16	17	18	19	20	21	22
23	24	25	26	27	28	29
30	31					

FEBRUARY 17 – FEBRUARY 23

2003

Presidents' Day

Mon 17

Tue 18

Wed 19

Thy 20

Fri 21

Washington's Birthday

Sat 22

Last Quarter Moon ☽

Sun 23

JANUARY						
S	M	T	W	T	F	S
			1	2	3	4
5	6	7	8	9	10	11
12	13	14	15	16	17	18
19	20	21	22	23	24	25
26	27	28	29	30	31	

FEBRUARY						
S	M	T	W	T	F	S
						1
2	3	4	5	6	7	8
9	10	11	12	13	14	15
16	17	18	19	20	21	22
23	24	25	26	27	28	

MARCH						
S	M	T	W	T	F	S
						1
2	3	4	5	6	7	8
9	10	11	12	13	14	15
16	17	18	19	20	21	22
23	24	25	26	27	28	29
30	31					

2003

Mon
24

Tue
25

Wed
26

Thu
27

Fri
28

St. David's Day (Wales)

Sat
1

New Moon ●

Sun
2

JANUARY						
S	M	T	W	T	F	S
			1	2	3	4
5	6	7	8	9	10	11
12	13	14	15	16	17	18
19	20	21	22	23	24	25
26	27	28	29	30	31	

FEBRUARY						
S	M	T	W	T	F	S
						1
2	3	4	5	6	7	8
9	10	11	12	13	14	15
16	17	18	19	20	21	22
23	24	25	26	27	28	

MARCH						
S	M	T	W	T	F	S
						1
2	3	4	5	6	7	8
9	10	11	12	13	14	15
16	17	18	19	20	21	22
23	24	25	26	27	28	29
30	31					

2003

Eight Hours Day (Tas.)

Labour Day (W.A.)

Mon 3

Tue 4

Ash Wednesday

Wed 5

Thu 6

Fri 7

International Women's Day

Sat 8

Sun 9

FEBRUARY						
S	M	T	W	T	F	S
						1
2	3	4	5	6	7	8
9	10	11	12	13	14	15
16	17	18	19	20	21	22
23	24	25	26	27	28	

MARCH						
S	M	T	W	T	F	S
						1
2	3	4	5	6	7	8
9	10	11	12	13	14	15
16	17	18	19	20	21	22
23	24	25	26	27	28	29
30	31					

APRIL						
S	M	T	W	T	F	S
		1	2	3	4	5
6	7	8	9	10	11	12
13	14	15	16	17	18	19
20	21	22	23	24	25	26
27	28	29	30			

MARCH 10 – MARCH 16

2003

Mon
10

Tue
11

Wed
12

Thu
13

Fri
14

Sat
15

Sun
16

FEBRUARY						
S	M	T	W	T	F	S
						1
2	3	4	5	6	7	8
9	10	11	12	13	14	15
16	17	18	19	20	21	22
23	24	25	26	27	28	

MARCH						
S	M	T	W	T	F	S
						1
2	3	4	5	6	7	8
9	10	11	12	13	14	15
16	17	18	19	20	21	22
23	24	25	26	27	28	29
30	31					

APRIL						
S	M	T	W	T	F	S
		1	2	3	4	5
6	7	8	9	10	11	12
13	14	15	16	17	18	19
20	21	22	23	24	25	26
27	28	29	30			

2003

St. Patrick's Day

Mon
17

Full Moon ○

Tue
18

Wed
19

Vernal Equinox 8:00 P.M. E.S.T.

Thu
20

Fri
21

Sat
22

Sun
23

FEBRUARY						
S	M	T	W	T	F	S
						1
2	3	4	5	6	7	8
9	10	11	12	13	14	15
16	17	18	19	20	21	22
23	24	25	26	27	28	

MARCH						
S	M	T	W	T	F	S
						1
2	3	4	5	6	7	8
9	10	11	12	13	14	15
16	17	18	19	20	21	22
23	24	25	26	27	28	29
30	31					

APRIL						
S	M	T	W	T	F	S
		1	2	3	4	5
6	7	8	9	10	11	12
13	14	15	16	17	18	19
20	21	22	23	24	25	26
27	28	29	30			

Otago Anniversary (N.Z.)

Last Quarter Moon ◑

Mon
24

Tue
25

Wed
26

Thu
27

Fri
28

Sat
29

Mothering Sunday (U.K.)

Daylight Saving Time begins (United Kingdom)

Sun
30

FEBRUARY						
S	M	T	W	T	F	S
						1
2	3	4	5	6	7	8
9	10	11	12	13	14	15
16	17	18	19	20	21	22
23	24	25	26	27	28	

MARCH						
S	M	T	W	T	F	S
						1
2	3	4	5	6	7	8
9	10	11	12	13	14	15
16	17	18	19	20	21	22
23	24	25	26	27	28	29
30	31					

APRIL						
S	M	T	W	T	F	S
		1	2	3	4	5
6	7	8	9	10	11	12
13	14	15	16	17	18	19
20	21	22	23	24	25	26
27	28	29	30			

MARCH 31 – APRIL 6

2003

Mon
31

New Moon ●

Tue
1

Wed
2

Thu
3

Fri
4

Sat
5

Daylight Saving Time begins (Canada & U.S.)

Sun
6

FEBRUARY
S	M	T	W	T	F	S
						1
2	3	4	5	6	7	8
9	10	11	12	13	14	15
16	17	18	19	20	21	22
23	24	25	26	27	28	

MARCH
S	M	T	W	T	F	S
						1
2	3	4	5	6	7	8
9	10	11	12	13	14	15
16	17	18	19	20	21	22
23	24	25	26	27	28	29
30	31					

APRIL
S	M	T	W	T	F	S
		1	2	3	4	5
6	7	8	9	10	11	12
13	14	15	16	17	18	19
20	21	22	23	24	25	26
27	28	29	30			

2003

Mon
7

Tue
8

First Quarter Moon ◗

Wed
9

Thu
10

Fri
11

Sat
12

Palm Sunday

Sun
13

M A R C H						
S	M	T	W	T	F	S
						1
2	3	4	5	6	7	8
9	10	11	12	13	14	15
16	17	18	19	20	21	22
23	24	25	26	27	28	29
30	31					

A P R I L						
S	M	T	W	T	F	S
		1	2	3	4	5
6	7	8	9	10	11	12
13	14	15	16	17	18	19
20	21	22	23	24	25	26
27	28	29	30			

M A Y						
S	M	T	W	T	F	S
				1	2	3
4	5	6	7	8	9	10
11	12	13	14	15	16	17
18	19	20	21	22	23	24
25	26	27	28	29	30	31

2003

Mon
14

Tue
15

Full Moon ○

Wed
16

Passover

Thu
17

Good Friday

Fri
18

Sat
19

Easter

Sun
20

MARCH						
S	M	T	W	T	F	S
						1
2	3	4	5	6	7	8
9	10	11	12	13	14	15
16	17	18	19	20	21	22
23	24	25	26	27	28	29
30	31					

APRIL						
S	M	T	W	T	F	S
		1	2	3	4	5
6	7	8	9	10	11	12
13	14	15	16	17	18	19
20	21	22	23	24	25	26
27	28	29	30			

MAY						
S	M	T	W	T	F	S
				1	2	3
4	5	6	7	8	9	10
11	12	13	14	15	16	17
18	19	20	21	22	23	24
25	26	27	28	29	30	31

2003

Easter Monday (Aust., Canada, N.Z., Rep. of Ireland & U.K.)

Mon 21

Earth Day

Tue 22

St. George's Day (England)

Last Quarter Moon ◑

Wed 23

Thu 24

National Arbor Day

Anzac Day (Aust. & N.Z.)

Fri 25

Sat 26

Ravenclaw
™

Sun 27

<table>
<tr><td colspan="7">MARCH</td></tr>
<tr><td>S</td><td>M</td><td>T</td><td>W</td><td>T</td><td>F</td><td>S</td></tr>
<tr><td></td><td></td><td></td><td></td><td></td><td></td><td>1</td></tr>
<tr><td>2</td><td>3</td><td>4</td><td>5</td><td>6</td><td>7</td><td>8</td></tr>
<tr><td>9</td><td>10</td><td>11</td><td>12</td><td>13</td><td>14</td><td>15</td></tr>
<tr><td>16</td><td>17</td><td>18</td><td>19</td><td>20</td><td>21</td><td>22</td></tr>
<tr><td>23</td><td>24</td><td>25</td><td>26</td><td>27</td><td>28</td><td>29</td></tr>
<tr><td>30</td><td>31</td><td></td><td></td><td></td><td></td><td></td></tr>
</table>

<table>
<tr><td colspan="7">APRIL</td></tr>
<tr><td>S</td><td>M</td><td>T</td><td>W</td><td>T</td><td>F</td><td>S</td></tr>
<tr><td></td><td></td><td>1</td><td>2</td><td>3</td><td>4</td><td>5</td></tr>
<tr><td>6</td><td>7</td><td>8</td><td>9</td><td>10</td><td>11</td><td>12</td></tr>
<tr><td>13</td><td>14</td><td>15</td><td>16</td><td>17</td><td>18</td><td>19</td></tr>
<tr><td>20</td><td>21</td><td>22</td><td>23</td><td>24</td><td>25</td><td>26</td></tr>
<tr><td>27</td><td>28</td><td>29</td><td>30</td><td></td><td></td><td></td></tr>
</table>

<table>
<tr><td colspan="7">MAY</td></tr>
<tr><td>S</td><td>M</td><td>T</td><td>W</td><td>T</td><td>F</td><td>S</td></tr>
<tr><td></td><td></td><td></td><td></td><td>1</td><td>2</td><td>3</td></tr>
<tr><td>4</td><td>5</td><td>6</td><td>7</td><td>8</td><td>9</td><td>10</td></tr>
<tr><td>11</td><td>12</td><td>13</td><td>14</td><td>15</td><td>16</td><td>17</td></tr>
<tr><td>18</td><td>19</td><td>20</td><td>21</td><td>22</td><td>23</td><td>24</td></tr>
<tr><td>25</td><td>26</td><td>27</td><td>28</td><td>29</td><td>30</td><td>31</td></tr>
</table>

2003

Mon
28

Tue
29

Wed
30

New Moon ●

Thu
1

Fri
2

Sat
3

HOGWARTS™ EXPRESS

Sun
4

MARCH						
S	M	T	W	T	F	S
						1
2	3	4	5	6	7	8
9	10	11	12	13	14	15
16	17	18	19	20	21	22
23	24	25	26	27	28	29
30	31					

APRIL						
S	M	T	W	T	F	S
		1	2	3	4	5
6	7	8	9	10	11	12
13	14	15	16	17	18	19
20	21	22	23	24	25	26
27	28	29	30			

MAY						
S	M	T	W	T	F	S
				1	2	3
4	5	6	7	8	9	10
11	12	13	14	15	16	17
18	19	20	21	22	23	24
25	26	27	28	29	30	31

MAY 5 – MAY 11

Mon 5

Tue 6

Wed 7

Thu 8

First Quarter Moon ◑

Fri 9

Sat 10

Mother's Day (Aust., Canada, N.Z. & U.S.)

Sun 11

APRIL						
S	M	T	W	T	F	S
		1	2	3	4	5
6	7	8	9	10	11	12
13	14	15	16	17	18	19
20	21	22	23	24	25	26
27	28	29	30			

MAY						
S	M	T	W	T	F	S
				1	2	3
4	5	6	7	8	9	10
11	12	13	14	15	16	17
18	19	20	21	22	23	24
25	26	27	28	29	30	31

JUNE						
S	M	T	W	T	F	S
1	2	3	4	5	6	7
8	9	10	11	12	13	14
15	16	17	18	19	20	21
22	23	24	25	26	27	28
29	30					

2003

_____

Mon 12

_____

Tue 13

_____

Wed 14

Full Moon ○

Thu 15

_____

Fri 16

_____

Sat 17

_____

Sun 18

_____

APRIL						
S	M	T	W	T	F	S
		1	2	3	4	5
6	7	8	9	10	11	12
13	14	15	16	17	18	19
20	21	22	23	24	25	26
27	28	29	30			

MAY						
S	M	T	W	T	F	S
				1	2	3
4	5	6	7	8	9	10
11	12	13	14	15	16	17
18	19	20	21	22	23	24
25	26	27	28	29	30	31

JUNE						
S	M	T	W	T	F	S
1	2	3	4	5	6	7
8	9	10	11	12	13	14
15	16	17	18	19	20	21
22	23	24	25	26	27	28
29	30					

MAY 19 – MAY 25

NORBERT

Victoria Day (Canada)

Mon 19

Tue 20

Wed 21

Last Quarter Moon ☾

Thu 22

Fri 23

Sat 24

Sun 25

APRIL						
S	M	T	W	T	F	S
		1	2	3	4	5
6	7	8	9	10	11	12
13	14	15	16	17	18	19
20	21	22	23	24	25	26
27	28	29	30			

MAY						
S	M	T	W	T	F	S
				1	2	3
4	5	6	7	8	9	10
11	12	13	14	15	16	17
18	19	20	21	22	23	24
25	26	27	28	29	30	31

JUNE						
S	M	T	W	T	F	S
1	2	3	4	5	6	7
8	9	10	11	12	13	14
15	16	17	18	19	20	21
22	23	24	25	26	27	28
29	30					

CHOCOLATE

2003

Memorial Day (observed)

Spring Holiday (U.K.)

Mon
26

Tue
27

Wed
28

Thu
29

Fri
30

New Moon ●

Sat
31

Sun
1

APRIL						
S	M	T	W	T	F	S
		1	2	3	4	5
6	7	8	9	10	11	12
13	14	15	16	17	18	19
20	21	22	23	24	25	26
27	28	29	30			

MAY						
S	M	T	W	T	F	S
				1	2	3
4	5	6	7	8	9	10
11	12	13	14	15	16	17
18	19	20	21	22	23	24
25	26	27	28	29	30	31

JUNE						
S	M	T	W	T	F	S
1	2	3	4	5	6	7
8	9	10	11	12	13	14
15	16	17	18	19	20	21
22	23	24	25	26	27	28
29	30					

2003

Queen's Birthday (N.Z.)

Holiday (Rep. of Ireland)

Mon
2

Tue
3

Wed
4

Thu
5

Fri
6

First Quarter Moon ◑

Pentecost

Whitsunday (Aust., N.Z. & U.K.)

MAY						
S	M	T	W	T	F	S
				1	2	3
4	5	6	7	8	9	10
11	12	13	14	15	16	17
18	19	20	21	22	23	24
25	26	27	28	29	30	31

JUNE						
S	M	T	W	T	F	S
1	2	3	4	5	6	7
8	9	10	11	12	13	14
15	16	17	18	19	20	21
22	23	24	25	26	27	28
29	30					

JULY						
S	M	T	W	T	F	S
		1	2	3	4	5
6	7	8	9	10	11	12
13	14	15	16	17	18	19
20	21	22	23	24	25	26
27	28	29	30	31		

2003

HOGWARTS

DRACO DORMIENS NUNQUAM TITILLANDUS

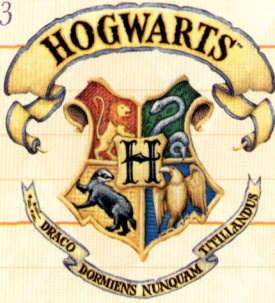

Queen's Birthday (Aust. except W.A.)

Mon
9

Tue
10

Wed
11

Thy
12

Fri
13

Flag Day

Full Moon ○

Sat
14

Father's Day (Canada, U.K. & U.S.)

Sun
15

MAY						
S	M	T	W	T	F	S
				1	2	3
4	5	6	7	8	9	10
11	12	13	14	15	16	17
18	19	20	21	22	23	24
25	26	27	28	29	30	31

JUNE						
S	M	T	W	T	F	S
1	2	3	4	5	6	7
8	9	10	11	12	13	14
15	16	17	18	19	20	21
22	23	24	25	26	27	28
29	30					

JULY						
S	M	T	W	T	F	S
		1	2	3	4	5
6	7	8	9	10	11	12
13	14	15	16	17	18	19
20	21	22	23	24	25	26
27	28	29	30	31		

Mon
16

Tue
17

Wed
18

Thy
19

Fri
20

Summer Solstice 3:10 P.M. E.D.T.

Last Quarter Moon ◑

Sat
21

Syn
22

MAY						
S	M	T	W	T	F	S
				1	2	3
4	5	6	7	8	9	10
11	12	13	14	15	16	17
18	19	20	21	22	23	24
25	26	27	28	29	30	31

JUNE						
S	M	T	W	T	F	S
1	2	3	4	5	6	7
8	9	10	11	12	13	14
15	16	17	18	19	20	21
22	23	24	25	26	27	28
29	30					

JULY						
S	M	T	W	T	F	S
		1	2	3	4	5
6	7	8	9	10	11	12
13	14	15	16	17	18	19
20	21	22	23	24	25	26
27	28	29	30	31		

June 23 – June 29

2003

Mon
23

St. Jean Baptiste Day (Quebec)

Tue
24

Wed
25

Thu
26

Fri
27

Sat
28

New Moon ●

Sun
29

MAY						
S	M	T	W	T	F	S
				1	2	3
4	5	6	7	8	9	10
11	12	13	14	15	16	17
18	19	20	21	22	23	24
25	26	27	28	29	30	31

JUNE						
S	M	T	W	T	F	S
1	2	3	4	5	6	7
8	9	10	11	12	13	14
15	16	17	18	19	20	21
22	23	24	25	26	27	28
29	30					

JULY						
S	M	T	W	T	F	S
		1	2	3	4	5
6	7	8	9	10	11	12
13	14	15	16	17	18	19
20	21	22	23	24	25	26
27	28	29	30	31		

Gryffindor

2003

Gryffindor

™

June 30 – July 6

Mon
30

Canada Day (Canada)

Tue
1

Wed
2

Thu
3

Independence Day

Fri
4

Sat
5

First Quarter Moon ◑

Sun
6

May						
S	M	T	W	T	F	S
				1	2	3
4	5	6	7	8	9	10
11	12	13	14	15	16	17
18	19	20	21	22	23	24
25	26	27	28	29	30	31

June						
S	M	T	W	T	F	S
1	2	3	4	5	6	7
8	9	10	11	12	13	14
15	16	17	18	19	20	21
22	23	24	25	26	27	28
29	30					

July						
S	M	T	W	T	F	S
		1	2	3	4	5
6	7	8	9	10	11	12
13	14	15	16	17	18	19
20	21	22	23	24	25	26
27	28	29	30	31		

2003

Mon
7

Tue
8

Wed
9

Thu
10

Fri
11

Sat
12

Full Moon ○

Sun
13

June

S	M	T	W	T	F	S
1	2	3	4	5	6	7
8	9	10	11	12	13	14
15	16	17	18	19	20	21
22	23	24	25	26	27	28
29	30					

July

S	M	T	W	T	F	S
		1	2	3	4	5
6	7	8	9	10	11	12
13	14	15	16	17	18	19
20	21	22	23	24	25	26
27	28	29	30	31		

August

S	M	T	W	T	F	S
					1	2
3	4	5	6	7	8	9
10	11	12	13	14	15	16
17	18	19	20	21	22	23
24	25	26	27	28	29	30
31						

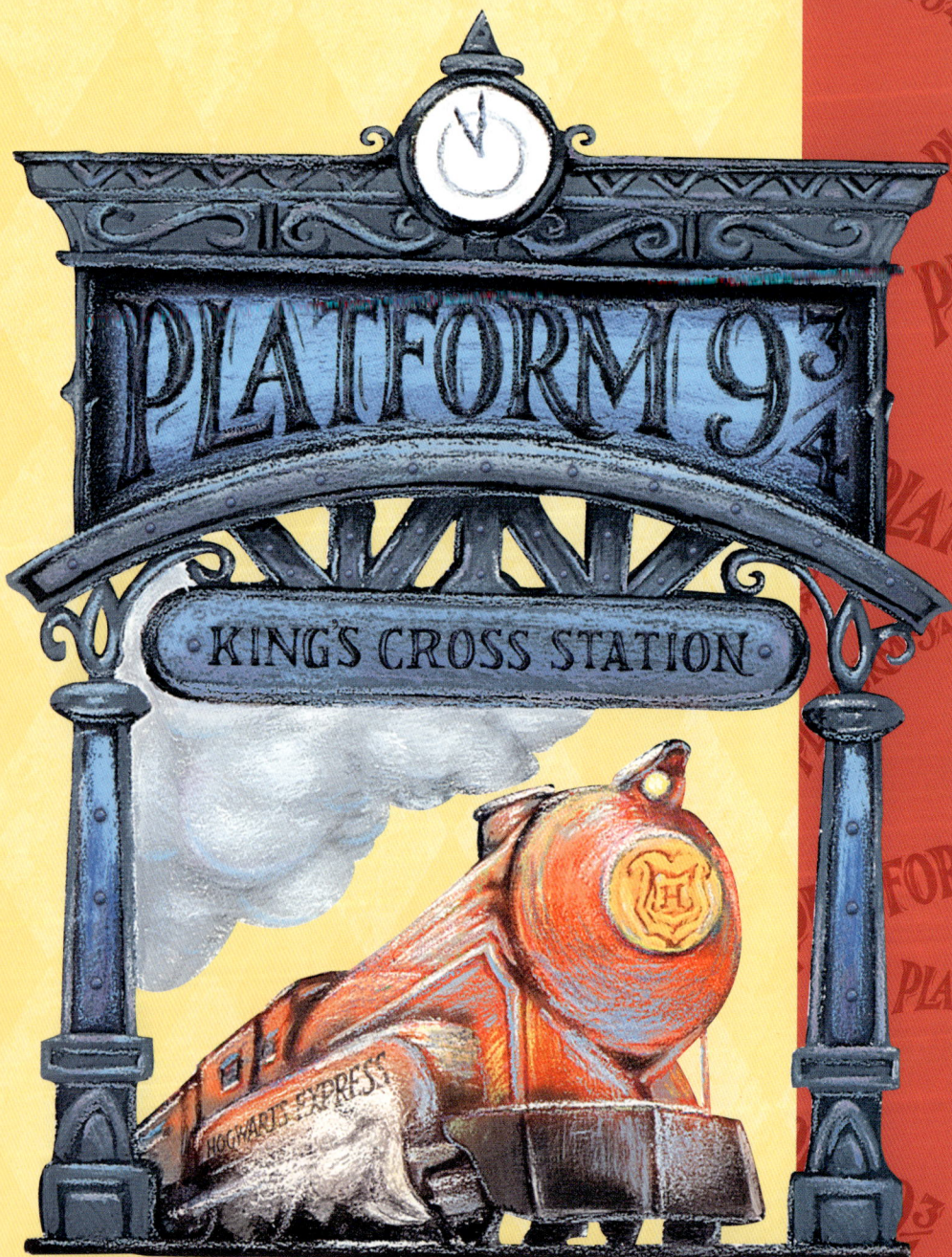

PLATFORM 9¾

KING'S CROSS STATION

HOGWARTS™ EXPRESS

JULY 14 – JULY 20

2003

Holiday (N. Ireland)

Mon 14

Tue 15

Wed 16

Thu 17

Fri 18

Sat 19

Sun 20

JUNE						
S	M	T	W	T	F	S
1	2	3	4	5	6	7
8	9	10	11	12	13	14
15	16	17	18	19	20	21
22	23	24	25	26	27	28
29	30					

JULY						
S	M	T	W	T	F	S
		1	2	3	4	5
6	7	8	9	10	11	12
13	14	15	16	17	18	19
20	21	22	23	24	25	26
27	28	29	30	31		

AUGUST						
S	M	T	W	T	F	S
					1	2
3	4	5	6	7	8	9
10	11	12	13	14	15	16
17	18	19	20	21	22	23
24	25	26	27	28	29	30
31						

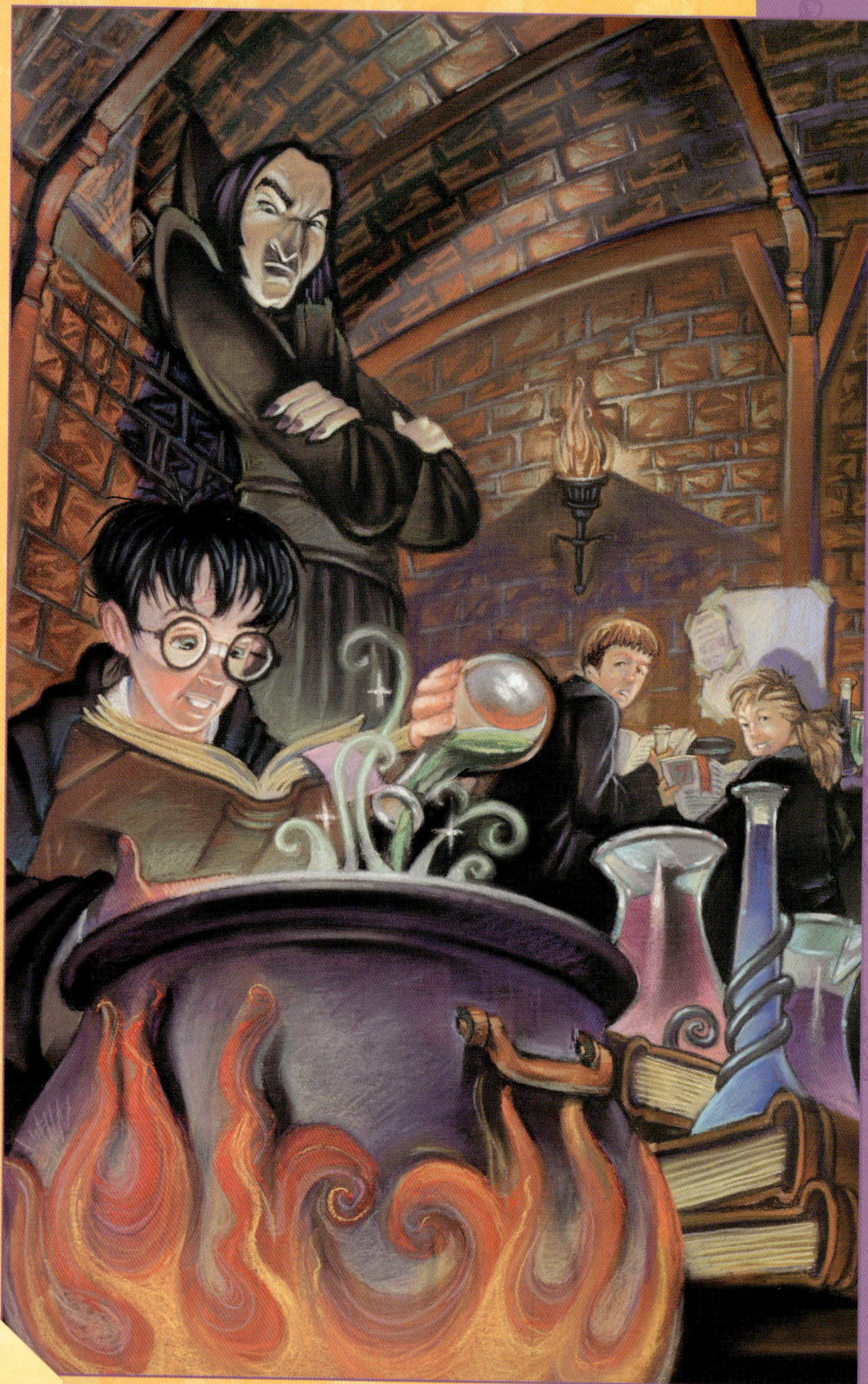

JULY 21 – JULY 27

2003

Last Quarter Moon ◑

Mon
21

Tue
22

Wed
23

Thu
24

Fri
25

Sat
26

Sun
27

JUNE						
S	M	T	W	T	F	S
1	2	3	4	5	6	7
8	9	10	11	12	13	14
15	16	17	18	19	20	21
22	23	24	25	26	27	28
29	30					

JULY						
S	M	T	W	T	F	S
		1	2	3	4	5
6	7	8	9	10	11	12
13	14	15	16	17	18	19
20	21	22	23	24	25	26
27	28	29	30	31		

AUGUST						
S	M	T	W	T	F	S
					1	2
3	4	5	6	7	8	9
10	11	12	13	14	15	16
17	18	19	20	21	22	23
24	25	26	27	28	29	30
31						

Mon
28

New Moon ●

Tue
29

Wed
30

Thu
31

Fri
1

Sat
2

SCABBERS™

Sun
3

JUNE						
S	M	T	W	T	F	S
1	2	3	4	5	6	7
8	9	10	11	12	13	14
15	16	17	18	19	20	21
22	23	24	25	26	27	28
29	30					

JULY						
S	M	T	W	T	F	S
		1	2	3	4	5
6	7	8	9	10	11	12
13	14	15	16	17	18	19
20	21	22	23	24	25	26
27	28	29	30	31		

AUGUST						
S	M	T	W	T	F	S
					1	2
3	4	5	6	7	8	9
10	11	12	13	14	15	16
17	18	19	20	21	22	23
24	25	26	27	28	29	30
31						

AUGUST 4 – AUGUST 10

2003

Holiday (Rep. of Ireland & Scotland)

Civic Holiday (Canada except Quebec)

Mon 4

First Quarter Moon ◑

Tue 5

Wed 6

Thu 7

Fri 8

Sat 9

Sun 10

JULY						
S	M	T	W	T	F	S
		1	2	3	4	5
6	7	8	9	10	11	12
13	14	15	16	17	18	19
20	21	22	23	24	25	26
27	28	29	30	31		

AUGUST						
S	M	T	W	T	F	S
					1	2
3	4	5	6	7	8	9
10	11	12	13	14	15	16
17	18	19	20	21	22	23
24	25	26	27	28	29	30
31						

SEPTEMBER						
S	M	T	W	T	F	S
	1	2	3	4	5	6
7	8	9	10	11	12	13
14	15	16	17	18	19	20
21	22	23	24	25	26	27
28	29	30				

2003

Mon
11

Full Moon ○

Tue
12

Wed
13

Thu
14

Fri
15

Sat
16

Sun
17

			July			
S	M	T	W	T	F	S
		1	2	3	4	5
6	7	8	9	10	11	12
13	14	15	16	17	18	19
20	21	22	23	24	25	26
27	28	29	30	31		

			August			
S	M	T	W	T	F	S
					1	2
3	4	5	6	7	8	9
10	11	12	13	14	15	16
17	18	19	20	21	22	23
24	25	26	27	28	29	30
31						

			September			
S	M	T	W	T	F	S
	1	2	3	4	5	6
7	8	9	10	11	12	13
14	15	16	17	18	19	20
21	22	23	24	25	26	27
28	29	30				

August 18 – August 24

Mon 18

Last Quarter Moon ◑

Tue 19

Wed 20

Thu 21

Fri 22

Sat 23

Sun 24

July						
S	M	T	W	T	F	S
		1	2	3	4	5
6	7	8	9	10	11	12
13	14	15	16	17	18	19
20	21	22	23	24	25	26
27	28	29	30	31		

August						
S	M	T	W	T	F	S
					1	2
3	4	5	6	7	8	9
10	11	12	13	14	15	16
17	18	19	20	21	22	23
24	25	26	27	28	29	30
31						

September						
S	M	T	W	T	F	S
	1	2	3	4	5	6
7	8	9	10	11	12	13
14	15	16	17	18	19	20
21	22	23	24	25	26	27
28	29	30				

2003

Late Summer Holiday (U.K. except Scotland)

Mon
25

Tue
26

New Moon ●

Wed
27

Thu
28

Fri
29

Sat
30

Sun
31

JULY						
S	M	T	W	T	F	S
		1	2	3	4	5
6	7	8	9	10	11	12
13	14	15	16	17	18	19
20	21	22	23	24	25	26
27	28	29	30	31		

AUGUST						
S	M	T	W	T	F	S
					1	2
3	4	5	6	7	8	9
10	11	12	13	14	15	16
17	18	19	20	21	22	23
24	25	26	27	28	29	30
31						

SEPTEMBER						
S	M	T	W	T	F	S
	1	2	3	4	5	6
7	8	9	10	11	12	13
14	15	16	17	18	19	20
21	22	23	24	25	26	27
28	29	30				

GRADE KEEPER

A = 4.0
B = 3.0
C = 2.0
D = 1.0
F = 0.0

Grade Point Average
To calculate Grade Point Average, divide total number of subjects by total grade point values.

Please note: These point values may differ slightly by school or state. Make sure you check with your instructor or guidance counselor before you calculate your GPA.

Subject	Date Grade	Date Grade	Date Grade	Date Grade	Date Grade	Date Grade	Date Grade

COMMONLY MISUSED WORDS

accept	to receive; to answer affirmatively (verb)
except	to leave out (verb); with the exclusion of (preposition)
addition	increase (noun)
edition	issue of a book (noun)
affect	to influence; to pretend (verb)
effect	a result, an influence, an impression (noun); to bring about (verb)
allude	to refer (verb)
elude	to avoid (verb)
angel	supernatural messenger (noun)
angle	corner (noun)
anxious	worried, uneasy (adjective)
eager	impatiently desirous (adjective)
bare	lacking covering, naked (adjective)
bear	to support, to hold up (verb)
board	piece of wood, food (room and board) (noun)
bored	uninterested (adjective)
capital	a city that is a seat of government; money; (noun)
capitol	the building in which a legislature meets (noun)
choose	to pick (verb)
chose	picked, past tense of choose (verb)
coarse	not fine (adjective)
course	path, unit of study (noun)
compare	to examine differences and similarities (verb)
contrast	to examine differences (verb)
complement	completer (noun), to provide balance (verb)
compliment	flattery (noun), to flatter (verb)
desert	to leave (verb), dry land (noun)
dessert	sweet course at end of meal (noun)
diagnosis	the identification of a disease or situation (noun)
prognosis	a prediction of the likely course of a disease or situation (noun)
emigrate	to leave a country to live elsewhere (verb)
immigrate	to enter a country to live there (verb)
forth	forward ahead (adjective)
fourth	number four (adjective)
gorilla	an ape (noun)
guerrilla	a member of an irregular military force (noun)
hear	listen and understand (verb)
here	in this place (adverb)
hole	a space, a void (noun)
whole	complete, intact (adjective)
illegible	not legible or decipherable (adjective)
unreadable	uninteresting, not worth reading (adjective)
imply	to express indirectly (transitive verb)
infer	to conclude from evidence, surmise (verb)
its	belonging to it (adjective)
it's	it is (contraction)

lay	to put; to set down (verb)
lie	to be or place oneself at rest in a recumbent position, recline (intransitive verb)
lightning	electricity caused by a storm (noun)
lightening	making or becoming lighter (verb)
lose	to misplace (verb)
loose	not tight (adjective)
notable	worthy, impressive (adjective)
notorious	widely known and ill-regarded (adjective)
passed	past tense of pass (verb)
past	previous (adjective)
peace	harmony; the absence of war (noun)
piece	part of a whole (noun)
pray	to implore; to address a deity (verb)
prey	a victim (noun)
precede	to go before (verb)
proceed	to continue (verb)
premier	first in status or importance, earliest (adjective)
premiere	the first public performance (noun)
principal	main (adjective); the person in charge (noun)
principle	a basic truth; a law (noun)
quiet	silent (adjective)
quit	to stop (verb)
quite	very (adverb)
right	correct (adjective)
rite	ceremony (noun)
stationary	not moving (adjective)
stationery	writing materials (noun)
statue	sculpture (noun)
stature	height, status (noun)
statute	law (noun)
taut	tight (adjective)
taught	past tense of teach (verb)
taunt	to tease (verb)
than	besides (preposition), as (conjunction)
then	at that time (adverb)
their	possessive form of they (pronoun)
there	in that place (adverb)
they're	they are (contraction)
through	in and out (preposition), finished (adjective)
thorough	complete (adjective)
to	toward (preposition)
too	or (adverb) also (adjective)
two	one plus one (adjective)
weather	atmospheric conditions (noun)
whether	if (conjunction)
whose	the possessive form of who (adjective)
who's	who is (contraction)
your	the possessive form of you (adjective)
you're	you are (contraction)

WEIGHTS & MEASURES

METRIC SYSTEM

LINEAR MEASURE

10 millimeter	1 centimeter
10 centimeters	1 decimeter
10 decimeters	1 meter
10 meters	1 decameter
10 decameters	1 hectometer
10 hectometers	1 kilometer

AREA MEASURE

100 sq millimeters	1 sq centimeter
10,000 sq centimeters	1 sq meter
1,000,000 sq millimeters	1 sq meter
100 sq meters	1 are (a)
100 ares	1 hectare (ha)
100 hectares	1 sq kilometer
1,000,000 sq meters	1 sq kilometer

VOLUME MEASURE

1 liter	0.001 cubic meter
10 milliliters	1 centiliter
10 centiliters	1 deciliter
10 deciliters	1 liter
10 liters	1 decaliter
10 decaliters	1 hectoliter
10 hectoliters	1 kiloliter

WEIGHT

10 milligrams	1 centigram
10 centigrams	1 decigram
10 decigrams	1 gram
10 grams	1 decagram
10 decagrams	1 hectogram
10 hectograms	1 kilogram
1,000 kilograms	1 metric ton

U.S. CUSTOMARY SYSTEM

LINEAR MEASURE

12 inches (in.)	1 foot
3 feet	1 yard
5 1/2 yards	1 rod
40 rods	1 furlong
8 furlongs	1 mile
3 land miles	1 league

AREA MEASURE

144 sq inches	1 sq foot
9 sq feet	1 sq yard
30 1/4 sq yards	1 sq rod
160 sq rods	1 acre
640 acres	1 sq mile
1 sq mile	1 section
36 sections	1 township

LIQUID MEASURE

3 tsp	1 tbsp
4 tbsp	1/4 cup
5 1/3 tbsp	1/3 cup
1 gill	1/2 cup
16 tbsp	1 cup
2 cups	1 pint
2 pints	1 quart
4 quarts	1 gallon

DRY MEASURE

2 pints	1 quart
8 quarts	1 peck
4 pecks	1 bushel

WEIGHT

27 $\frac{11}{32}$ grains	1 dram
16 drams	1 ounce
16 ounces	1 pound
100 pounds	1 hundredweight
20 hundredweight	1 ton
2,000 pounds	1 ton

CONVERSIONS

From	To	Multiply by	From	To	Multiply by	From	To	Multiply by
centimeters	inches	.3937	kilograms	grams	1,000	meters	yards	1.093
centimeters	feet	.0328	kilograms	ounces	35.274	miles	feet	5,280
centimeters	meters	.01	kilograms	pounds	2.2046	miles	yards	1,760
centimeters	millimeters	10	kilometers	feet	3,281	miles	kilometers	1.609
feet	inches	12	kilometers	meters	1,000	ounces	grams	28.35
feet	meters	.3048	kilometers	miles	.621	ounces	pounds	.0625
feet	miles	.001894	kilometers	yards	1,093	ounces	kilograms	.028
feet	yards	.3333	liters	cups	4.226	pounds	grams	453.59
gallons	pints	8	liters	pints	2.113	pounds	ounces	16
gallons	liters	3.785	liters	gallons	.264	pounds	kilograms	.454
gallons	quarts	4	liters	milliliters	1,000	quarts	pints	2
grams	ounces	.035	liters	quarts	1.057	quarts	liters	.946
grams	pounds	.002	meters	centimeters	100	quarts	gallons	.25
grams	kilograms	.001	meters	feet	3.281	yards	inches	36
inches	centimeters	2.54	meters	inches	39.37	yards	feet	3
inches	feet	.0833	meters	kilometers	.001	yards	meters	.914
inches	meters	.0254	meters	miles	.0006214	yards	miles	.0005682
inches	yards	.0278	meters	millimeters	1,000			

Commonly Misspelled Words

a lot	believe	disappoint	hero	nickel	realtor	surprise
absence	beneficial	disapprove	heroes	ninety	received	swimming
acceptable	beneficiary	discussion	horizontal	notary public	recommend	
accidentally	benefit	disease	humorous	noticeable	rehearsal	technicality
accommodate	breath	dividend		nuclear	religious	technique
accuracy	breathe	division	illogical	nuisance	remember	tendency
acknowledgment	brilliant	doesn't	imaginary		repetition	tension
(acknowledgement)	bureaucracy	don't	immediately	occasion	representative	themselves
acquaint	business	during	independent	occurrence	responsibility	therefore
acquaintance			indispensable	occurring	responsible	thorough
acquire	calendar	effect	individual	omission	restaurant	thought
across	career	efficient	influence	opportunity	reversible	thousandth
actually	carefully	eighth	influential	oppressed	rhythm	through
adapt	catalog	eligible	inoculate	optimistic		Thursday
adequately	(catalogue)	embarrassed	intelligent		sacrifice	together
admission	category	envelope	interest	paid	said	tomorrow
adolescent	cemetery	environment	interruption	parallel	sandwich	tragedy
advertise	certain	epitome	invariably	parameter	satellite	transferred
affect	character	equipment	irresistible	paroled	Saturday	traveled
against	chief	equipped		particle	scarcity	truly
aggravate	choose	escape	January	particularly	schedule	Tuesday
all right	clothes	especially	jewelry	pastime	secretary	twelfth
(alright)	committee	exaggerate	judgment	peculiar	seize	tyranny
although	compare	excel	(judgement)	performance	separate	
always	competition	excellent		perimeter	September	unanimous
amateur	complement	except	knowledgeable	permanent	signature	undoubtedly
among	completely	excite		permissible	significance	unfortunate
amount	compliment	exercise	label	pleasant	significant	until
analyze	condemned	existence	laboratory	poison	sincerely	used to
annually	conscience	expense	latter	politician	skiing	useful
anticipated	conscious	experiment	leisurely	pollute	society	usually
apparent	controlled	experience	length	possession	soluble	
appearance	controversial	explanation	license	possible	someone	vacuum
appropriate	convenient		literature	practically	souvenir	vertical
argument	couldn't	facsimile	lonely	precede	speech	villain
around	country	familiar	luxury	precedent	stationary	visibility
article	courtesy	fascinate		preceding	stationery	vitamin
assassination	cried	fascist	magnificent	preference	statistics	
athletic	criticized	favorite	maintain	prescription	straight	Wednesday
attacked	curiosity	February	maintenance	privilege	strategy	weird
attendance		finally	maneuver	probably	strength	woman
audience	dealt	financially	marriage	procedure	strictly	(women)
author	decide	forty	maybe	proceed	stubbornness	writing
auxiliary	definitely	fulfill	meant	professor	studied	written
awkward	description		minutes	pronunciation	studies	
	develop	government	missile	propaganda	studying	yield
bargain	diagnosis	governor	mortgage	proposal	suburban	
battery	diagonal	guarantee	mountain	psychology	succeed	
beautiful	difference	guaranteed	mysterious	psychiatry	success	
beginning	different	happened	necessary	questionnaire	summarized	
belief	disappear	height	negotiate	quipped	superintendent	

Name _____   Phone _____
Address _____   E-mail _____
_____   Pager _____

Name _____   Phone _____
Address _____   E-mail _____
_____   Pager _____

Name _____   Phone _____
Address _____   E-mail _____
_____   Pager _____

Name _____   Phone _____
Address _____   E-mail _____
_____   Pager _____

Name _____   Phone _____
Address _____   E-mail _____
_____   Pager _____

Name _____   Phone _____
Address _____   E-mail _____
_____   Pager _____

Name _____   Phone _____
Address _____   E-mail _____
_____   Pager _____

Name _____   Phone _____
Address _____   E-mail _____
_____   Pager _____

Name _____   Phone _____
Address _____   E-mail _____
_____   Pager _____

Name

Phone

Address

E-mail

Pager

Name

Phone

Address

E-mail

Pager

Name

Phone

Address

E-mail

Pager

Name

Phone

Address

E-mail

Pager

Name

Phone

Address

E-mail

Pager

Name

Phone

Address

E-mail

Pager

Name

Phone

Address

E-mail

Pager

Name

Phone

Address

E-mail

Pager

Name

Phone

Address

E-mail

Pager

BIRTHDAYS & SPECIAL OCCASIONS

EVENT   DATE